Little Koko Bear
and His Socks

by Qiusheng Zhang • illustrated by Kaiyun Xu

Little Koko Bear loved socks.

Striped socks, polka-dot socks, socks with hearts—Koko Bear loved them all.

"Socks! Socks! Socks!" sang Koko Bear.

"Socks are what I like to wear.

Red socks, blue socks, I don't care."

"Do you like my brand-new pair?"

Little Koko Bear spent all his time thinking about socks, looking at socks, and trying on socks.

He was so busy with his socks that he didn't have any time left to make friends.

But there was ONE thing Koko Bear didn't like about his socks.

He didn't like washing them.

So, after he wore a pair of socks, little Koko Bear would toss them under his bed.

After a while, there was a big pile of dirty, stinky socks under his bed.

Then one morning, Koko Bear woke up to find that he didn't have a single clean pair of socks to wear.

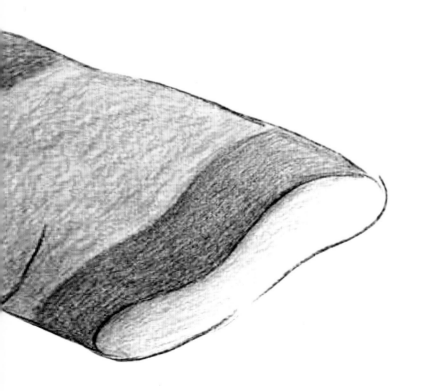
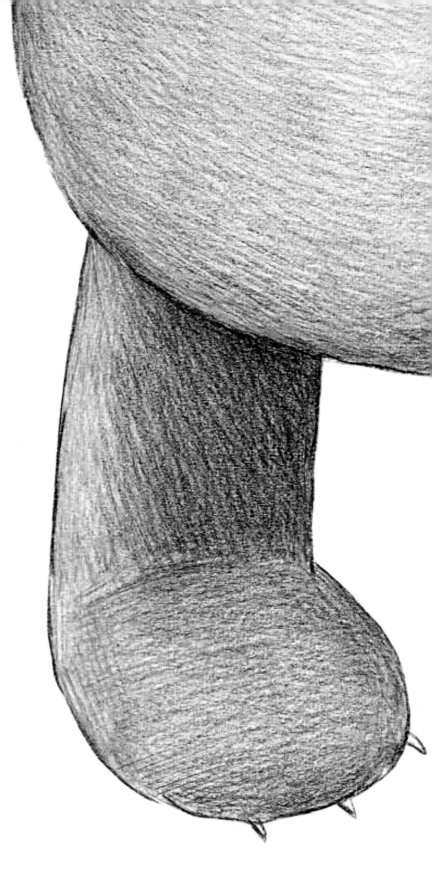

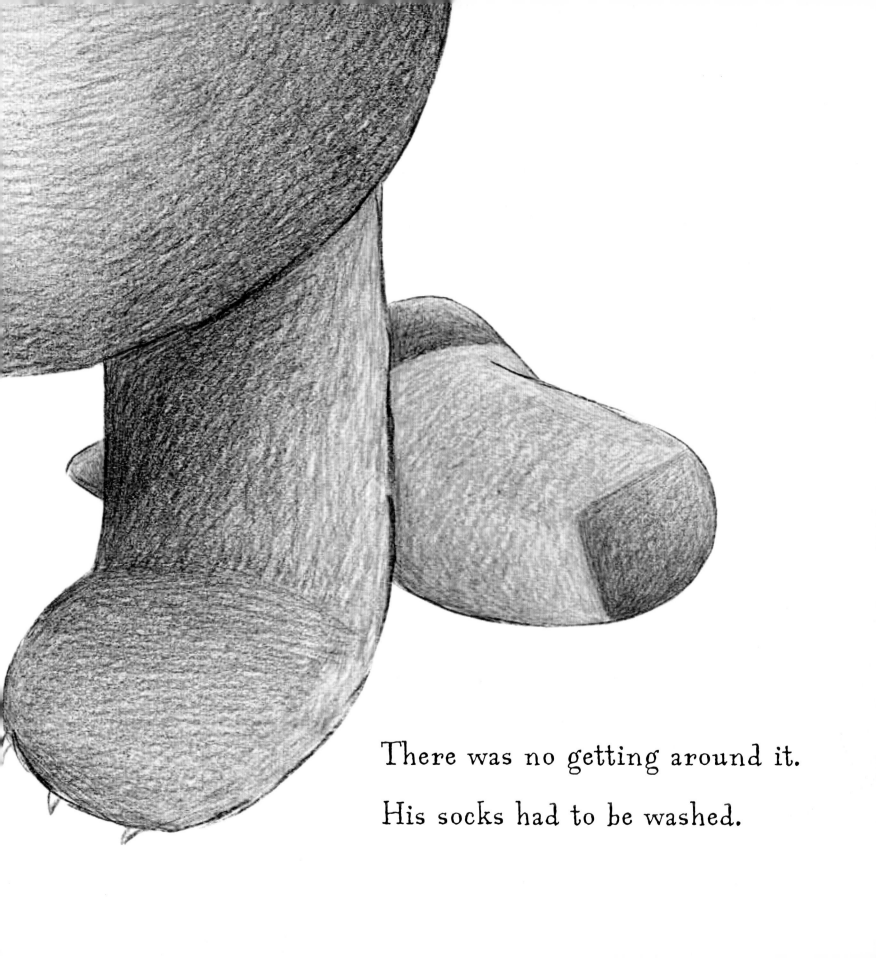

There was no getting around it.

His socks had to be washed.

Little Koko Bear put all his socks in a basket and carried them down to the river.

Dirty socks, dirty socks, everywhere. Not a single sock to wear.

When he was done washing them, Koko Bear hung up his socks to dry. All that work had made him very tired. He lay down under a tree and fell fast asleep.

While Koko Bear slept, a friendly badger passed by.

"Look!" she said to herself. "This little bear is selling socks. I don't want to wake him up, but I do need socks. I will take some and pay with the cookies I baked this morning."

So the badger took a few pairs of socks and left behind her delicious cookies.

Koko Bear slept on. A while later,
a cheerful chimpanzee wandered by.

"Oh, look at that!" said the chimpanzee.
"This little bear is selling socks.
I don't want to wake him, but I do
need socks. I'll take some and leave
my fresh apples."

So the chimp took a pair of socks and left
his crisp, juicy apples for Koko Bear.

Little Koko Bear snoozed on. Soon an artist passed by.

"How beautiful!" the artist said. "These socks are like works of art! I don't want to wake him, but I do need socks. I'll take some and paint his picture as payment."

So the artist painted a picture of little Koko Bear and left it next to the cookies and the apples. Then he went away, taking two pairs of socks with him.

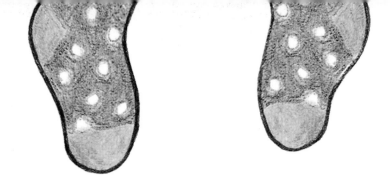

Soon, all the animals in the forest heard that a sleeping bear was selling cheerful, colorful socks. Everyone rushed to get a pair or two.

They all left behind something special for Koko Bear.

Later that afternoon, Koko Bear woke up.
He opened his eyes. He looked up and down.
He looked all around.

Where were his socks?

Only two pairs of socks were left on the line.

Where were his polka-dot socks?

Where were his heart socks?

Little Koko Bear wanted to cry.

But then he noticed all the wonderful gifts.

Koko Bear packed the two pairs of socks in his basket along with all the gifts and headed back home.

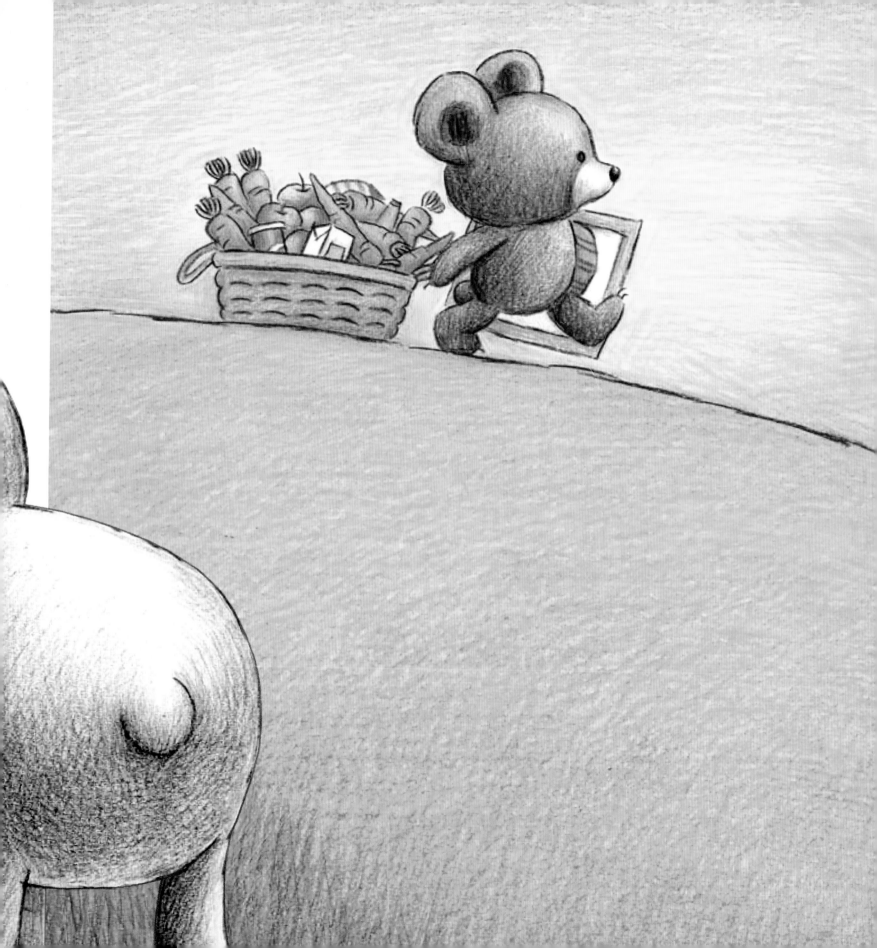

Now that Koko Bear had only two pairs of socks, he had to wash them at the river almost every day. But he didn't mind. He no longer hated washing socks. Instead, he enjoyed being at the river and talking to the animals he met. He made many new friends.

Little Koko Bear invited his new friends to come over.

He was proud of his house now that there weren't any smelly socks under his bed.

Happy, happy Koko Bear!
Now he has

clean socks to wear.

He's got tasty snacks to share.

And plenty of

good friends who care.